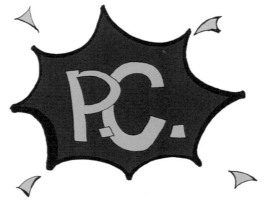

# P.C.

## Penny Farthing
## goes to school
## TO TEACH STRANGER DANGER

Author
## Wendy Roberts

Illustrator
## Amy Bradley

*AuthorHouse™ UK Ltd.*
*500 Avebury Boulevard*
*Central Milton Keynes, MK9 2BE*
*www.authorhouse.co.uk*
*Phone: 08001974150*

*First published by AuthorHouse 3/2/2011*

*ISBN: 978-1-4520-0112-8 (sc)*

*This book is printed on acid-free paper.*

authorHOUSE®

Penny helps her children, Rose and Anne, get ready for school.

They have their breakfast and then they all walk to school together.

After Penny has dropped the twins off at school she continues the rest of her journey to the near by police station.

Penny is a police officer called Police Constable Penny Farthing.

Sometimes Penny drives to work however today she has walked.

Police Constable Penny arrives at the Newtown police station.

Penny wears a police uniform. She puts on her cravat, her epaulets and her radio. She also puts on her stab proof vest to protect herself.

Penny puts her belt around her waist and clips it into place.

The belt Penny wears has lots of kit upon it. It has a first aid pouch in case anybody is hurt when she is out and about on foot patrol.

Penny also has silver handcuffs which she puts on people if they try to run away from her. She also has a baton to protect herself.

Today Police Constable Penny has agreed to talk to the children at the local school about PERSONAL SAFETY AND STRANGER DANGER.

Penny turns on her police radio and clips it onto her shirt. She tells the controller on the other end of the radio where she is going today.

Today Penny is driving a marked police car to the school.

The marked police car has stripes down the sides and the back so she can be seen when driving it in the dark or bad weather.

When Penny arrives at the school the children rush over to see her. She shows the car to the children who are very excited to see it.

# WHEN the ScHOOL BeLL Sounds
children run into line to get ready to walk into school.

Penny walks into the classroom with the children of class one along with the class teacher Mrs Smith.

Penny stands at the front of the classroom and the children sit around her feet listening to what she has to say. They are excited to see Penny as she is so kind.

Penny asks the children if they have ever played at the local park, lots o children put their hands up.

If a person approaches you when you are on your own you must not go off with them.

Penny asks

"What should you do if you get lost in the shops?"

A little boy with lots of curly hair and freckles called Noel puts his hand up and excitedly says

"I Know Penny my mummy says I should go into the nearest shop and tell the lady behind the counter I have lost my mummy"

Penny smiles and says

"Thats a great answer Noel thats what you could do if you get lost, well done."

If you get lost and can see a police officer, you could go up to them and tell them you are lost. They will help you to find your mummy, daddy, or grown up helper.

Penny asks the children

"Can you think of anyone else who may be able to help lost children find their parents or grown up helper?"

If you get lost when you are out with a grown up you could try and find

A shop assistant in A shop,

A security guard,

or community support officer,

OR PERHAPS A POLICE OFFICER

and tell them you have lost your grown up.
They will help you and try to find your grown up

The children invite Penny to join them for their snacks and milk.

Penny says "Thank you for my snack it is time for me to go back to the police station, thank you for being so well behaved, it was great to come and talk to you all."

Penny drives her marked police car back to Newtown police station and parks it in the stations back yard.

Penny takes her kit out of the car and walks back into the police station.

Penny puts her kit away for the night and she says goodnight to the controller on her radio before switching it off and putting it into her locker.

The following day Penny is working she is on duty in her uniform walking through the town centre when she notices a young child from the primary school.

The child is wallking towards her with her mummy her name is Jenny.

Jennys mum is looking very relieved and says to Penny "I can't thank you enough Penny for going into the school yesterday and talking about stranger danger and personal safety."

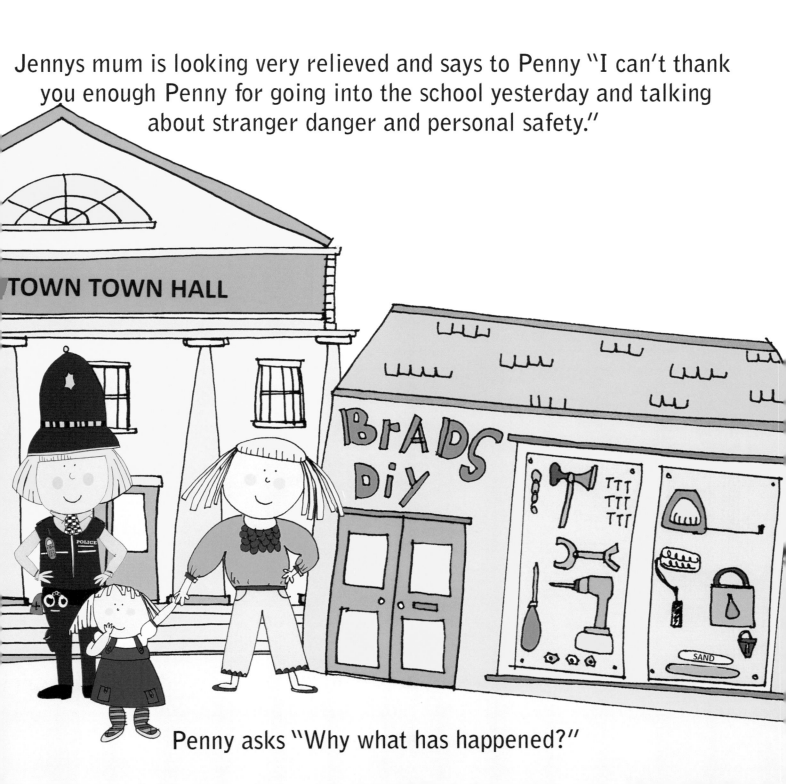

Penny asks "Why what has happened?"

Jenny's mum replies "Jenny got split up from me in the busy shopping centre and I couldn't find her.....

she remembered what you said to her yesterday in class she went straigh up to a member of staff in the clothes shop and told them she had lost her mummy."

"The shop keeper called the security guard who came to them. They found me looking for her a short while later."

"Jenny"

Jenny's mummy said " I can't thank you enough Penny, I think all children should be taught at school about stranger danger and personal safety."

Penny agrees with Jenny's mummy and says "Yes all children should be taught about this, it could help keep lots of children safe."

Penny was really pleased Jenny listened so well in class yesterday.

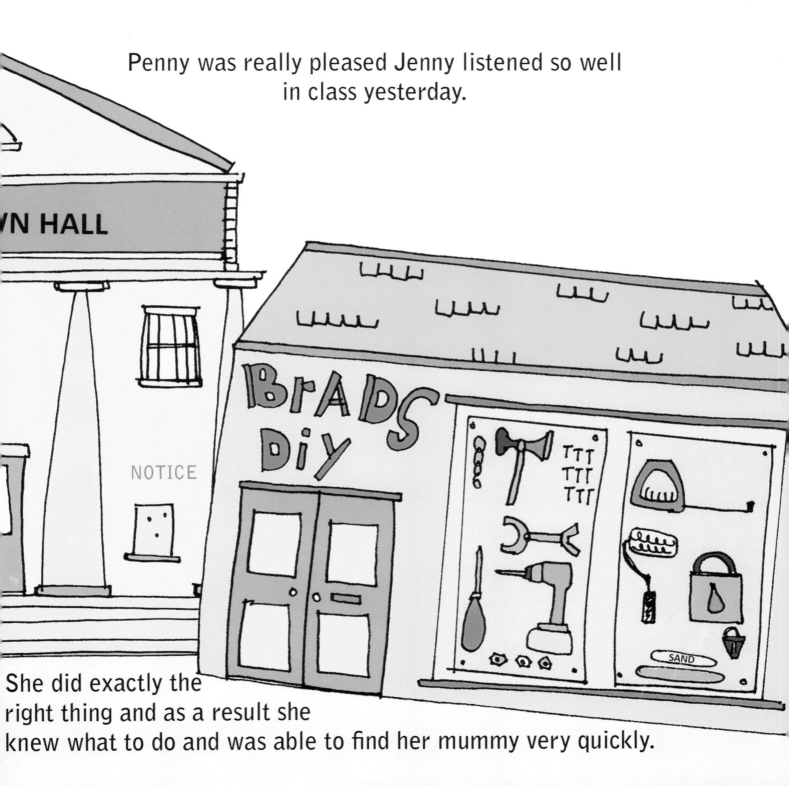

She did exactly the right thing and as a result she knew what to do and was able to find her mummy very quickly.

Its nearly time for Penny to go home so she starts to walk back to the station.

Penny puts her kit away and says goodnight to the controller.

Penny leaves the police station for the night and
walks to collect her children from school

they all walk home together.